This book belongs to

_____

THE TAILOR OF GLOUCESTER

BEATRIX POTTER

ILLUSTRATED BY
ALLEN ATKINSON

AN ARIEL BOOK

BANTAM BOOKS
TORONTO   NEW YORK   LONDON   SYDNEY

THE TAILOR OF GLOUCESTER
A Bantam Book
December 1983

Design: Iris Bass
Art Direction: Armand Eisen

Acknowledgment: The illustrator would like to thank Hal Hochvert
and Anne Greenberg for their fine work on the production of this book,
with special thanks to the editors Ron Buehl and Lu Ann Walther

Bantam Books are published by Bantam Books, Inc. Its trademark, con-
sisting of the words "Bantam Books" and the portrayal of a rooster, is
Registered in U.S. Patent and Trademark Office and in other countries.
Marca Registrada, Bantam Books, Inc., 666 Fifth Avenue, New York,
New York 10103

Printing and binding by
Printer, industria gráfica S.A.   Provenza, 388   Barcelona-25
Depósito legal B. 29083-1983
PRINTED IN SPAIN
0   9   8   7   6   5   4   3   2   1

The art is dedicated
to my friend
Pete R.

IN THE TIME OF swords and periwigs and full-skirted coats with flowered lappets—when gentlemen wore ruffles, and gold-laced waistcoats of paduasoy and taffeta—there lived a tailor in Gloucester.

He sat in the window of a little shop in Westgate Street, cross-legged on a table, from morning till dark.

THE TAILOR OF GLOUCESTER

All day long while the light lasted he sewed and snippeted, piecing out his satin and pompadour, and lute-string; stuffs had strange names, and were very expensive in the days of the Tailor of Gloucester.

THE TAILOR OF GLOUCESTER

But although he sewed fine silk for his neighbours, he himself was very, very poor—a little old man in spectacles, with a pinched face, old crooked fingers, and a suit of thread-bare clothes.

He cut his coats without waste, according to his embroidered cloth; they were very small ends and snippets that lay about upon the table—"Too narrow breadths for nought—except waistcoats for mice," said the tailor.

THE TAILOR OF GLOUCESTER

One bitter cold day near Christmas-time the tailor began to make a coat—a coat of cherry-coloured corded silk embroidered with pansies and roses, and a cream-coloured satin waistcoat—trimmed with gauze and green worsted chenille—for the Mayor of Gloucester.

The tailor worked and worked, and he talked to himself. He measured the silk, and turned it round and round, and trimmed it into shape with his shears; the table was all littered with cherry-coloured snippets.

THE TAILOR OF GLOUCESTER

"No breadth at all, and cut on the cross; it is no breadth at all; tippets for mice and ribbons for mobs! for mice!" said the Tailor of Gloucester.

When the snow-flakes came down against the small leaded window-panes and shut out the light, the tailor had done his day's work; all the silk and satin lay cut out upon the table.

THE TAILOR OF GLOUCESTER

There were twelve pieces for the coat and four pieces for the waistcoat; and there were pocket flaps and cuffs, and buttons all in order. For the lining of the coat there was fine yellow taffeta; and for the button-holes of the waistcoat, there was cherry-coloured twist. And everything was ready to sew together in the morning, all measured and sufficient—except that there was wanting just one single skein of cherry-coloured twisted silk.

THE TAILOR OF GLOUCESTER

The tailor came out of his shop at dark, for he did not sleep there at nights; he fastened the window and locked the door, and took away the key. No one lived there at  night but little brown mice, and they run in and out without any keys!

For behind the wooden wainscots of all the old houses in Gloucester, there are little mouse staircases and secret trapdoors; and the mice run from house to

house through those long narrow passages; they can run all over the town without going into the streets.

THE TAILOR OF GLOUCESTER

But the tailor came out of his shop, and shuffled home through the snow. He lived quite near by in College Court, next the doorway to College Green; and although it was not a big house, the tailor was so poor he only rented the kitchen.

He lived alone with his cat; it was called Simpkin.

Now all day long while the tailor was out at work, Simpkin kept house by himself; and he also was fond of the mice, though he gave them no satin for coats!

"Miaw?" said the cat when the tailor opened the door. "Miaw?"

THE TAILOR OF GLOUCESTER

THE TAILOR OF GLOUCESTER

The tailor replied—"Simpkin, we shall make our fortune, but I am worn to a ravelling. Take this groat (which is our last fourpence) and Simpkin, take a china pipkin; buy a penn'orth of bread, a penn'orth of milk and a penn'orth of sausages. And oh, Simpkin, with the last penny of our fourpence buy me one penn'orth of cherry-coloured silk. But do not lose the last penny of the fourpence, Simpkin, or I am undone and worn to a thread-paper, for I have NO MORE TWIST."

Then Simpkin again said, "Miaw?" and took the groat and the pipkin, and went out into the dark.

The tailor was very tired and beginning to be ill. He sat down by the hearth and talked to himself about that wonderful coat.

"I shall make my fortune—to be cut bias—the Mayor of Gloucester is to be married on Christmas Day in the morning, and he hath ordered a coat and an embroidered waistcoat—to be lined with yellow taffeta—and the taffeta sufficeth; there is no more left over in snippets than will serve to make tippets for mice—"

THE TAILOR OF GLOUCESTER

THE TAILOR OF GLOUCESTER

Then the tailor started; for suddenly, interrupting him, from the dresser at the other side of the kitchen came a number of little noises—

Tip tap, tip tap, tip tap tip!

"Now what can that be?" said the Tailor of Gloucester, jumping up from his chair. The dresser was covered with crockery and pipkins, willow pattern plates, and tea-cups and mugs.

THE TAILOR OF GLOUCESTER

The tailor crossed the kitchen, and stood quite still beside the dresser, listening, and peering through his spectacles. Again from under a tea-cup, came those funny little noises—

Tip tap, tip tap, tip tap tip!

"This is very peculiar," said the Tailor of Gloucester; and he lifted up the tea-cup which was upside down.

THE TAILOR OF GLOUCESTER

Out stepped a little live lady mouse, and made a curtsey to the tailor! Then she hopped away down off the dresser, and under the wainscot.

The tailor sat down again by the fire, warming his poor cold hands, and mumbling to himself—

"The waistcoat is cut out from peach-coloured satin—tambour stitch and rose-buds in beautiful floss silk. Was I wise to entrust my last fourpence to Simpkin? One-and-twenty button-holes of cherry-coloured twist!"

THE TAILOR OF GLOUCESTER

But all at once, from the dresser, there came other little noises:

Tip tap, tip tap, tip tap tip!

"This is passing extraordinary!" said the Tailor of Gloucester, and turned over another tea-cup, which was upside down.

Out stepped a little gentleman mouse, and made a bow to the tailor!

And then from all over the dresser came a chorus of little tappings, all sounding together, and answering one another, like watch-beetles in an old worm-eaten window-shutter—

THE TAILOR OF GLOUCESTER

THE TAILOR OF GLOUCESTER

Tip tap, tip tap, tip tap tip!
And out from under tea-cups and from
under bowls and basins, stepped other
and more little mice who
hopped away down
off the dresser
and under the
wainscot.

The tailor sat down, close over the fire, lamenting—"One-and-twenty button-holes of cherry-coloured silk! To be finished by noon of Saturday: and this is Tuesday evening. Was it right to let loose those mice, undoubtedly the property of Simpkin? Alack, I am undone, for I have no more twist!"

The little mice came out again, and listened to the tailor; they took notice of the pattern of that wonderful coat. They whispered to one another about the taffeta lining, and about little mouse tippets.

And then all at once they all ran away together down the passage behind the wainscot, squeaking and calling to one another, as they ran from house to house;

THE TAILOR OF GLOUCESTER

and not one mouse was left
in the tailor's kitchen when
Simpkin came back with
the pipkin of milk!

THE TAILOR OF GLOUCESTER

Simpkin opened the door and bounced in, with an angry "G-r-r-miaw!" like a cat that is vexed: for he hated the snow, and there was snow in his ears, and snow in his collar at the back of his neck. He put down the loaf and the sausages upon the dresser, and sniffed.

"Simpkin," said the tailor, "where is my twist?"

But Simpkin set down the pipkin of milk upon the dresser, and looked suspiciously at the tea-cups. He wanted his supper of little fat mouse!

31

THE TAILOR OF GLOUCESTER

"Simpkin," said the tailor, "where is my TWIST?"

But Simpkin hid a little parcel privately in the tea-pot, and spit and growled at the tailor; and if Simpkin had been able to talk, he would have asked: "Where is my MOUSE?"

THE TAILOR OF GLOUCESTER

"Alack, I am undone!" said the Tailor of Gloucester, and went sadly to bed.

All that night long Simpkin hunted and searched through the kitchen, peeping into cupboards and under the wainscot, and into the tea-pot where he had hidden that twist; but still he found never a mouse!

THE TAILOR OF GLOUCESTER

Whenever the tailor muttered and talked in his sleep, Simpkin said "Miaw-ger-r-w-s-s-ch!" and made strange horrid noises, as cats do at night.

For the poor old tailor was very ill with a fever, tossing and turning in his four-post bed; and still in his dreams he mumbled—"No more twist! no more twist!"

THE TAILOR OF GLOUCESTER

All that day he was ill, and the next day, and the next; and what should become of the cherry-coloured coat? In the tailor's shop in Westgate Street the embroidered silk and satin lay cut out upon the table—one-and-twenty button-holes—and who should come to sew them, when the window was barred, and the door was fast locked?

THE TAILOR OF GLOUCESTER

 But that does not hinder the little brown mice; they run in and out without any keys through all the old houses in Gloucester!

Out of doors the market folks went trudging through the snow to buy their geese and turkeys, and to bake their Christmas pies; but there would be no Christmas dinner for Simpkin and the poor old Tailor of Gloucester.

THE TAILOR OF GLOUCESTER

The tailor lay ill for three days and nights; and then it was Christmas Eve, and very late at night. The moon climbed up over the roofs and chimneys, and looked down over the gateway into College Court. There were no lights in the windows, nor any sound in the houses; all the city of Gloucester was fast asleep under the snow.

37

And still
Simpkin wanted
his mice, and he
mewed as he
stood beside
the four-post
bed.

THE TAILOR OF GLOUCESTER

But it is in the old story that all the beasts can talk, in the night between Christmas Eve and Christmas Day in the morning (though there are very few folk that can hear them, or know what it is that they say).

When the Cathedral clock struck twelve there was an answer—like an echo of the chimes—and Simpkin heard it, and came out of the tailor's door, and wandered about in the snow.

THE TAILOR OF GLOUCESTER

From all the roofs and gables and old wooden houses in Gloucester came a thousand merry voices singing the old Christmas rhymes—all the old songs that ever I heard of, and some that I don't know, like Whittington's bells.

First and loudest the cocks cried out: "Dame, get up, and bake your pies!"

"Oh, dilly, dilly, dilly!" sighed Simpkin.

And now in a garret there were lights and sounds of dancing, and cats came from over the way.

THE TAILOR OF GLOUCESTER

"Hey, diddle, diddle, the cat and the fiddle! All the cats in Gloucester— except me," said Simpkin.

Under the wooden eaves the starlings and sparrows sang of Christmas pies; the jack-daws woke up in the Cathedral tower; and although it was the middle of the night the throstles and robins sang; the air was quite full of little twittering tunes.

But it was all rather provoking to poor hungry Simpkin!

THE TAILOR OF GLOUCESTER

THE TAILOR OF GLOUCESTER

Particularly he was vexed with some little shrill voices from behind a wooden lattice. I think that they were bats, because they always have very small voices—especially in a black frost, when they talk in their sleep, like the Tailor of Gloucester.

They said something mysterious that sounded like—

"Buz, quoth the blue fly; hum, quoth the bee;
Buz and hum they cry, and so do we!"

and Simpkin went away shaking his ears as if he had a bee in his bonnet.

THE TAILOR OF GLOUCESTER

From the tailor's shop in Westgate came a glow of light; and when Simpkin crept up to peep in at the window it was full of candles. There was a snippeting of scissors, and snappeting of thread; and little mouse voices sang loudly and gaily—

"Four-and-twenty tailors
   Went to catch a snail,
   The best man amongst them
   Durst not touch her tail;
   She put out her horns
   Like a little kyloe cow,
Run, tailors, run! or she'll have you all e'en now!"

THE TAILOR OF GLOUCESTER

Then without a pause the little mouse voices went on again—

> "Sieve my lady's oatmeal,
> Grind my lady's flour,
> Put it in a chestnut,
> Let it stand an hour—"

"Mew! Mew!" interrupted Simpkin, and he scratched at the door. But the key was under the tailor's pillow, he could not get in.

The little mice only laughed, and tried another tune—

THE TAILOR OF GLOUCESTER

"Three little mice sat down to spin,
Pussy passed by and she peeped in.
What are you at, my fine little men?
Making coats for gentlemen.
Shall I come in and cut off your threads?
Oh, no, Miss Pussy, you'd bite off our heads!"

"Mew! Mew!" cried Simpkin. "Hey diddle dinketty?" answered the little mice—

"Hey diddle dinketty, poppetty pet!
The merchants of London they wear scarlet;
Silk in the collar, and gold in the hem,
So merrily march the merchantmen!"

THE TAILOR OF GLOUCESTER

They clicked their thimbles to mark the time, but none of the songs pleased Simpkin; he sniffed and mewed at the door of the shop.

"And then I bought
   A pipkin and a popkin,
   A slipkin and a slopkin,
   All for one farthing—

and upon the kitchen dresser!" added the rude little mice.

THE TAILOR OF GLOUCESTER

THE TAILOR OF GLOUCESTER

"Mew! scratch! scratch!" scuffled Simpkin on the window-sill; while the little mice inside sprang to their feet, and all began to shout at once in little twittering voices: "No more twist! No more twist!" And they barred up the window shutters and shut out Simpkin.

But still through the nicks in the shutters he could hear the click of thimbles, and little mouse voices singing—

"No more twist! No more twist!"

Simpkin came away from the shop and went home, considering in his mind. He found the poor old tailor without fever, sleeping peacefully.

Then Simpkin went on tip-toe and took a little parcel of silk out of the tea-pot, and looked at it in the moonlight; and he felt quite ashamed of his badness compared with those good little mice!

THE TAILOR OF GLOUCESTER

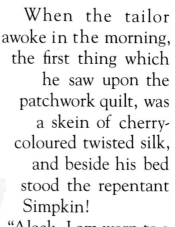

When the tailor awoke in the morning, the first thing which he saw upon the patchwork quilt, was a skein of cherry-coloured twisted silk, and beside his bed stood the repentant Simpkin!

"Alack, I am worn to a ravelling," said the Tailor of Gloucester, "but I have my twist!"

THE TAILOR OF GLOUCESTER

The sun was shining on the snow
when the tailor got up and dressed, and
came out into the street with
Simpkin running before
him.

THE TAILOR OF GLOUCESTER

The starlings
whistled on the chimney
stacks, and the throstles and robins
sang—but they sang their own little
noises, not the words they had sung in
the night.

"Alack," said the tailor, "I have my twist; but no more strength—nor time— than will serve to make me one single button-hole; for this is Christmas Day in the Morning! The Mayor of Gloucester shall be married by noon—and where is his cherry-coloured coat?"

He unlocked the door of the little shop in Westgate Street, and Simpkin ran in, like a cat that expects something.

But there was no one there! Not even one little brown mouse!

THE TAILOR OF GLOUCESTER

The boards were swept clean; the little ends of thread and the little silk snippets were all tidied away, and gone from off the floor.

But upon the table—oh joy! the tailor gave a shout—there, where he had left plain cuttings of silk—there lay the most beautifullest coat and embroidered satin waistcoat that ever were worn by a Mayor of Gloucester.

THE TAILOR OF GLOUCESTER

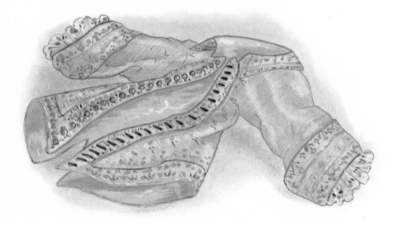

There were roses and pansies upon the facings of the coat; and the waistcoat was worked with poppies and corn-flowers.

Everything was finished except just one single cherry-coloured button-hole, and where that button-hole was wanting there was pinned a scrap of paper with these words—in little teeny weeny writing—

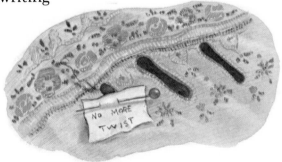

THE TAILOR OF GLOUCESTER

And from then began the luck of the Tailor of Gloucester; he grew quite stout, and he grew quite rich.

He made the most wonderful waistcoats for all the rich merchants of Gloucester, and for all the fine gentlemen of the country round.

Never were seen such ruffles, or such embroidered cuffs and lappets! But his button-holes were the greatest triumph of it all.

THE TAILOR OF GLOUCESTER

The stitches of those button-holes were so neat—*so* neat—I wonder how they could be stitched by an old man in spectacles, with crooked old fingers, and a tailor's thimble.

The stitches of those button-holes were so small—*so* small— they looked as if they had been made by little mice!

W9-CHO-953

YOU MUST REMEMBER THIS

1975

MILESTONES, MEMORIES,
TRIVIA AND FACTS, NEWS EVENTS,
PROMINENT PERSONALITIES &
SPORTS HIGHLIGHTS OF THE YEAR

TO :

FROM :

MESSAGE :

selected and researched
by
mary a. pradt

WARNER ⓦ TREASURES ™

PUBLISHED BY WARNER BOOKS

A TIME WARNER COMPANY

Warner Books, Inc.
1271 Avenue of the Americas
New York, New York 10020

Warner Treasures is a
trademark of Warner Books, Inc.

Ⓦ A Time Warner Company

DESIGN:
CAROL BOKUNIEWICZ DESIGN
PRINTED IN SINGAPORE
FIRST PRINTING : MAY 1995
10 9 8 7 6 5 4 3 2 1
ISBN : 0-446-91052-X

New York City narrowly averted financial collapse. The New York *Daily News*'s famous headline:

"ford to new york: drop dead."

A SENATE INVESTIGATION, AS WELL AS ONE BY A PRESIDENTIAL COMMISSION, ISSUED REPORTS OF WIDESPREAD DOMESTIC SPYING BY THE CIA AND ALLEGED ASSASSINATION PLOTS ABROAD.

In September, Ford was twice the target of assassination attempts – first by Lynette **squeaky fromme,** a Charles Manson follower, and later by Sara Jane Moore, an activist.

newsreel

President Gerald Ford was in command at the top. Watergate sentences were being handed down. John Mitchell, former attorney general, and former White House aides H. R. Haldeman and John D. Ehrlichman were sentenced to jail time in February for their roles in the Watergate break-in of June 17, 1972, and the subsequent cover-up that brought down the Nixon presidency.

Saigon and the rest of South Vietnam finally fell to the Communists. More than 100,000 Vietnamese refugees were evacuated to the U.S. In April, more than 100 Vietnamese orphans, part of an airlift of 243 headed for American homes, were killed when their American Air Force plane crashed after take-off from Saigon.

headlines

American Astronauts and Soviet Cosmonauts linked up in space. The Apollo and Soyuz spacecraft docked, and the three men aboard each spent time in the others' craft. They performed scientific experiments, traded gifts, and flew in formation for two orbits.

The United Nations
declared it the
Year of the Women

Britain's Conservative Party
elected its first woman leader,
margaret thatcher

Sony introduced a videotape recorder intended for the masses, not for professional broadcasters: think this invention would ever catch on?

PAY $!?!
CABLE TV

began to make its first impact on television, as Hollywood movies were offered to subscribers for the first time without commercial interruption. Although cable TV had been around for years, to get broadcast signals out to the boondocks, Home Box Office was the first to offer premium programming nearly–new films and a few special events for a monthly fee.

patty hearst

THE HEIRESS WHO WAS KID-NAPPED BY THE RADICAL SYMBIONESE LIBERATION ARMY IN FEB. 1974, BUT BECAME A SYMPATHETIC ACCOMPLICE TO BANK ROB-BERY, WAS APPREHENDED ON SEPTEMBER 18, 1975.

cultural
milestones

A CHORUS LINE
BEGAN ITS REIGN
AS BROADWAY'S
LONGEST-RUNNING
MUSICAL.

'75

7

television

JOHNNY CARSON WAS KING OF LATE-NIGHT TV FOR NBC. ("NIGHTLINE" DID NOT YET EXIST.) NBC HAD "TODAY," "TONIGHT," AND "TOMORROW," SO THEY DECIDED TO STAKE OUT THE WEEKEND: "SATURDAY NIGHT LIVE" WAS NBC'S LATE-NIGHT COMEDY FORAY, ALMOST IMMEDIATELY SUCCESSFUL. FINALLY, THERE WAS AN EXCUSE TO STAY HOME ON SATURDAY NIGHT.

In 1975 there were 68.5 million TV households in the U.S., according to A.C. Nielsen figures. The percentage of American homes with TV had reached 97.

top-rated shows:

1. "All in the Family" (CBS)
2. "Rich Man, Poor Man" (ABC)
3. "Laverne and Shirley" (ABC)
4. "Maude" (CBS)
5. "The Bionic Woman" (ABC)
6. "Phyllis" (CBS)
7. "Sanford & Son" (NBC)
8. "Rhoda" (CBS)
9. "The Six Million Dollar Man" (ABC)
10. "ABC Monday Night Movie" (ABC)

NOTE THE PROLIFERATION OF SITCOMS AND SPINOFFS (BOTH VALERIE HARPER'S "RHODA" AND CLORIS LEACHMAN'S "PHYLLIS" WERE NEIGHBORS OF MARY TYLER MOORE).

milestones

elizabeth taylor remarried
richard burton October 10,
after 14 months of divorce.

divorce of the year
ann landers, SYNDICATED ADVICE COLUMNIST,
JULY 1 ANNOUNCED IN HER COLUMN THAT SHE
WAS DIVORCING AFTER 36 YEARS OF MARRIAGE.

elvis presley
TURNED 40 ON
JANUARY 8, 1975.

born in 1975

DREW BARRYMORE actress, was born in L.A. February 22, 1975. Onscreen since the age of seven, she has acknowledged that she had substance-abuse problems before she was 10.

SEAN ONO LENNON son of John Lennon and Yoko Ono, was born October 9. John called his son "the All-American boy" because Sean helped him attain legal U.S. residency after John Lennon spent three years fighting deportation.

1975 MARKS THE END OF THE "BABY BUST," OR GENERATION X, THE PERIOD OF MANY FEWER BIRTHS THAN THE PRECEDING "BABY BOOM."

DEATHS

Julian "Cannonball" Adderley, jazz saxophonist, died August 8.

Josephine Baker the American-born singer and dancer who introduced "le jazz hot" to Paris and became the personification of black talent on two continents, died April 12, 1975, in Paris.

Susan Hayward Oscar-winning actress who earned more than 50 feature film credits in a 34-year movie career, died March 14, 1975.

Ozzie Nelson, radio and television personality and popular bandleader, who portrayed the stereotypical American father for 22 years on radio and TV, died June 3, 1975.

Aristotle Socrates Onassis, Greek shipping magnate and second husband of Jacqueline Bouvier Kennedy, whom he had married in 1968, died March 15. In 1977, a negotiated settlement would give the widow $20 million from the Onassis estate, more than double what she would have received under the terms of his will.

Rod Serling, creator of the sci-fi/fantasy series "The Twilight Zone," died June 28, 1975.

Walker Evans, photographer and educator, died April 10, 1975.

75

hit music

1. **love will keep us together** Captain & Tenille
2. **fly, robin, fly** Silver Convention
3. **island girl** Elton John
4. **he don't love you (like i love you)** Tony Orlando & Dawn
5. **bad blood** Neil Sedaka
6. **rhinestone cowboy** Glenn Campbell
7. **philadelphia freedom** Elton John Band
8. **that's the way** KC & the Sunshine Band
9. **jive talkin** Bee Gees
10. **fame** David Bowie

In October 1975, to the chagrin of both, both *Time* and *Newsweek* had Bruce Springsteen on the cover in the same week. Bruce was labeled "the future of rock" with the release of the "Born to Run" album.

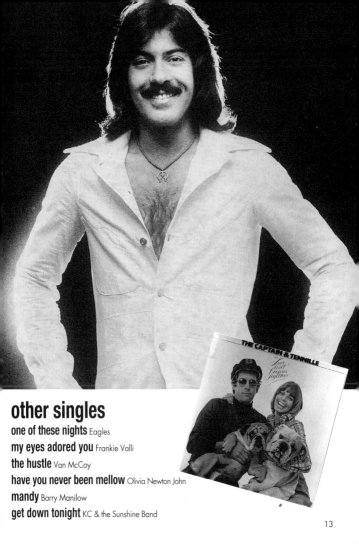

other singles

one of these nights Eagles

my eyes adored you Frankie Valli

the hustle Van McCoy

have you never been mellow Olivia Newton John

mandy Barry Manilow

get down tonight KC & the Sunshine Band

bestselling

fiction

1. **ragtime**
   e. l. doctorow

2. **the moneychangers**
   arthur hailey

3. **curtain**
   agatha christie

4. **looking for
   mr. goodbar**
   judith rossner

5. **the choirboys**
   joseph wambaugh

6. **the eagle has landed**
   jack higgins

7. **the greek treasure :
   a biographical novel
   of henry and sophia
   schliemann**
   irving stone

8. **the great train
   robbery**
   michael crichton

9. **shogun**
   james clavell

10. **humboldt's gift**
    saul bellow

IN 1975 HARDCOVER FICTION
SALES WERE DOWN. *RAGTIME*
WON THE FIRST NATIONAL
BOOK CRITICS CIRCLE FICTION
AWARD AND SET A RECORD
WHEN BANTAM BOUGHT
PAPERBACK RIGHTS FOR
$1,850,000.

books

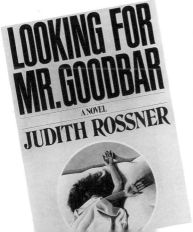

Billy Graham's *Angels: God's Secret Agents* was the runaway nonfiction bestseller. The rest of the list was dominated by books on meditation, self-assertion, diet, exercise, and other self-help.

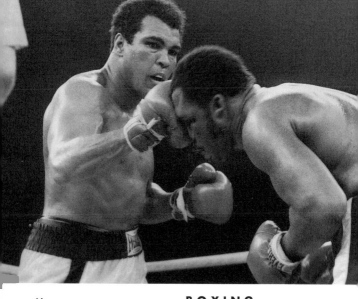

Arthur Ashe scored a stunning upset over Jimmy Connors at Wimbledon.

BOXING

MUHAMMAD ALI WON THE "THRILLA IN MANILA" OCTOBER 1 BY A TKO; HE SURVIVED 14 GRUELING ROUNDS WITH CHALLENGER JOE FRAZIER.

casey stengel, former baseball player, coach, manager, and inventor of a personal idiom called "stengelese," died september 29, 1975. The Yankees won ten pennants and seven world championships under his management.

Martina Navratilova,18, the Czech tennis star, was granted asylum in the U.S. in September and received permanent resident status in October.

Oklahoma was the nation's #1 college team for the second straight year.

SUPER BOWL: THE STEELER DEFENSE HELD FRAN TARKENTON AND THE MINNESOTA VIKINGS TO A STANDSTILL IN NEW ORLEANS JANUARY 12, LEADING PITTSBURGH TO A 16-6 VICTORY.

sports

In one of the most exciting World Series in history, the Cincinnati Reds outdueled the Boston Red Sox, defeating the Sox 4-3 in the final game.

The Golden State Warriors won the NBA championship.

shampoo STARRING WARREN BEATTY AS A HOLLYWOOD HAIRDRESSER, COMMENTED WRYLY ON THE SIXTIES.

academy awards

One Flew Over the Cuckoo's Nest dominated Oscar night. It was named Best Picture. **Jack Nicholson** established himself as a major star with his Oscar-winning Best Actor performance in **Cuckoo's Nest**. His co-star, **Louise Fletcher,** won Best Actress honors for her role as the insane-asylum nurse. **Milos Forman,** who directed, also won an Oscar.

jaws WAS THE BIGGEST WORD IN HOLLYWOOD'S VOCABU-LARY. WITHIN FIVE MONTHS OF ITS U.S. AND CANADIAN RELEASE, IT HAD REALIZED $95 MILLION AT THE BOX OFFICE, BECOMING THE TOP-GROSS-ING FILM IN HISTORY. IT WAS DIRECTED BY 27-YEAR-OLD STEVEN SPIELBERG, WHOSE ONLY PREVIOUS SUCCESS WAS THE SUGARLAND EXPRESS.

tommy, DIRECTED BY KEN RUSSELL, WAS BASED ON THE ROCK OPERA BY THE WHO. WITH ROGER DALTREY, ANN-MARGRET, OLIVER REED, AND ELTON JOHN.

ROBERT ALTMAN'S SPRAWLING **NASHVILLE** WAS CRITICALLY ACCLAIMED. **LOVE AND DEATH**, BY WOODY ALLEN, STARRED HIMSELF AND DIANE KEATON. BARBRA STREISAND STARRED IN **FUNNY LADY,** WITH JAMES CAAN AND OMAR SHARIF FEATURED.

movies

Stanley Kubrick unveiled his lush **Barry Lyndon** for the holiday season.

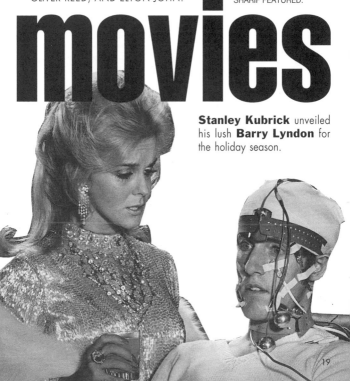

19

75'

Detroit suffered the lowest model production run since 1961.

The American auto industry was mired in one of its worst slumps since World War II. The Big Three were forced to offer rebates to get consumers to buy new cars. Chrysler was first, in January 1975, to offer rebates of $200 - $400 on new cars. Value-minded buyers went for such cars as the Oldsmobile Cutlass and the compact Buick Apollo. The Ford Division star was the

wheels

new Granada compact. Its twin was the Mercury Monarch; Monarch and Granada were priced at $4,000 and up. Even Cadillac produced a "compact" Seville, priced at $13,000+.

SENSE FOR TODAY. Chevrolet

MONTE CARLO.
Its special ability: making you feel good.

The 1975 Monte Carlo makes you feel good, not just about the way it looks and drives, but about *yourself*. About your taste, because Monte Carlo styling is clean, honest, unpretentious. And about your judgment, because Monte Carlo is an authentic road car; a car neatly sized, impressively engineered, and one enjoying all the efficiency benefits listed on the following page.

Move to Monte Carlo. It feels good.

Monte Carlo Landau

CAMARO.
There's no law against driving with a smile on your face.

For 1975, we've left Camaro's styling pretty much alone—on the theory that when a car looks this good, you shouldn't mess around with it.

So we widened the rear window a bit, added some new colors, put on some new identification, then turned our attention to mechanical things. (See back page.)

The result is a sporty compact which, like before, looks like a million and moves like it looks. But now Camaro's more efficient, more sensible, and an even smarter choice than ever.

Camaro Type LT Coupe

IMPALA.
All the benefits of full size, plus new economies, too.

One reason Impala has been America's favorite car for so many years is the roominess it provides for so many people's driving needs. Impala for 1975 still provides a lot of room, ride, comfort and usable trunk space for the thousands of people who can't settle for less than a full-size car. Plus Chevrolet's new Efficiency System that makes Impala a more economical, sensible car that will save you money every mile you drive. We've taken a car already recognized as the Great American Value and made it even more valuable for 1975.

Impala Custom Coupe

women's clothes

The major fashion trends for 1975 were denim and China (the country, not the pottery). The craze for jeans continued unabated. The new leg was the "cigarette," narrow of leg and rolled up mid-calf over boots. Another popular jean look was the two-zipper, straight-leg jean that closed with two side front zippers instead of a fly front. A straw bag from Mainland China was an important acces-

THE T-SHIRT, EMBLAZONED WITH A SLOGAN, A LOGO, A PHOTO—FINALLY CAME OF AGE AS THE UBIQUITOUS ARTICLE OF CLOTHING IN 1975. DENIM WAS BRUSHED, STREAKED, PREWASHED, EMBROIDERED, BEADED, BLEACHED, OR STUDDED.

The earth shoe was popular with both sexes

sory. Mandarin collars, quilted "coolie" jackets, and other classic Asian touches began to appear in sportswear. Sweaters were "in" with a vengeance — preferably something ethnic, such as Mexican, Peruvian, Icelandic, or Native American.

fashion

men's fashion

Leisure suits were still popular, but the three-piece suit, especially with a reversible vest, was a fashion contender. Jewelry for men was big business. Neck chains with ivory or silver sharks' teeth, silver and turquoise, and scarabs.

final factoid

An unemployed California adman named Gary Dahl was talking with some barroom buddies about the hassles of pet ownership, and Dahl spun a story about his pet rock. Dahl then came up with a funny owner's manual, gathered some beach stones, and had a friend design a quaint box for the pet, with a little bed of straw. He got financing, and within a few months, the Pet Rock was selling tens of thousands a day. The entrepreneur did hundreds of interviews for papers, magazines, radio and TV. He was the guest of "The Tonight Show" twice. Rocks could be taught to roll over, especially on hills, to heel, and to play dead. Dahl became a millionaire. This craze was criticized as totally frivolous merchandising, but it seemed to be just what the country needed after Vietnam and Watergate.

**the pet rock
is the unlikely
best-selling
holiday gift.**

'75